ANIMAL
✚ RESCUE CENTER

By

The
Porch
Puppy

This series is for my riding friend Shelley,
who cares about all animals.

ANIMAL
RESCUE CENTER

Other titles in the series:

The Unwanted Puppy

The Home-alone Kitten

The Injured Fox Kit

The Homeless Foal

The Runaway Rabbit

The Lost Duckling

The Abandoned Hamster

The Sad Pony

tiger tales
5 River Road, Suite 128, Wilton, CT 06897
Published in the United States 2018
Originally published in Great Britain 2008
as *The Doorstep Puppy* by the Little Tiger Group
Text copyright © 2008, 2018 Jenny Oldfield
Interior illustrations copyright © 2018 Artful Doodlers
Cover illustration copyright © 2018 Anna Chernyshova
Images courtesy of www.shutterstock.com
ISBN-13: 978-1-68010-426-4
ISBN-10: 1-68010-426-8
Printed in China
STP/1800/0187/0218
All rights reserved
10 9 8 7 6 5 4 3 2 1

For more insight and activities, visit us at www.tigertalesbooks.com

Contents

ANIMAL MAGIC
RESCUE CENTER

 HOME

ADOPT

 FRIENDS

MEET THE ANIMALS IN NEED OF A HOME!

DOTTY

Dotty would love a warm home and family of her own. Can you give her the care she needs?

COCOA AND PEANUT

Two fluffy youngsters who need a home together. Are you willing to comb and cuddle them?

MURPHY

A lively boy, good with children. He's recovering from an operation, so he needs plenty of TLC.

SITE SEARCH

 NEWS

 HELP US

 CONTACT

 DONATE!

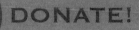

EBONY

Ebony is a lap cat. Curl up for lots of cozy nights with this beautiful girl—purrfect!

ROCKY

Don't let his tough act fool you—Rocky's a shy dog who will follow wherever you go.

ACE

Ace's elderly owner has been taken into the hospital. Can you give him a new home?

Chapter One
Puppy Playtime

"Caleb, come and look at this!" On the Monday before Christmas, Ella Harrison called her brother into the yard at Animal Magic Rescue Center.

Caleb stuck his head out of the stable block. "I can't right now. I've got to finish mucking out Rosie's stable."

"It will only take a minute. Just come and look at this puppy playing with the yard brush." Ella couldn't help laughing. The tiny black-and-white Border collie had clamped her jaws onto the bristles and was growling and tugging the entire thing into the middle of the frosty yard. "She thinks she's really fierce!"

"Yap!" The pup wriggled and rolled, covering herself in white frost and almost whacking herself with the broom handle.

Though he was busy mucking out, Caleb came to take a look. "Who does she belong to?"

"Mr. Price brought her in with three other puppies. Mom has given them their first set of injections. This one made a run for it. You're an escapee, aren't you?" Ella said, crouching down and petting the puppy. "But you're very, *very* cute."

"Not bad," Caleb said, picking the puppy up and dusting her off. "We can find a home for you, no problem. And your brothers and sisters, too."

The lively puppy licked Caleb's hand and wriggled free. Once more she stalked the yard brush, then pounced. "Yip-yap-yap!"

"Beautiful!" Ella sighed. It was one of her dreams to have a puppy of her own, but her mom and dad had a strict rule about not adopting any of the pets who came into the center.

"Come back here, you little monkey!" A voice called from the doorway into the reception area. It was the puppy's owner, Joe Price, who lived up at Lakeview Farm.

At last Ella persuaded the puppy to let go of the brush. She carried her across to the farmer. "What's her name?" Ella asked, handing the puppy over.

"This one is named Holly." The farmer half smiled as he grasped the wriggling puppy. "There's one other girl in the litter. Her name is Ivy. Holly and Ivy— Christmas puppies. Get it?" A huge grin spread across his face. "The dogs are Jingle and Kringle."

"Holly, Ivy, Jingle, and Kringle." Caleb repeated the names. "Would you like us to put them on the Animal Magic website?"

Mr. Price shook his head. "No need for

that. I'm hoping to turn three of these puppies into working dogs. Jingle is going to Zach Larsen over at Stonybrook."

"We know Zach," Ella broke in. "He helped us set up a small animals sanctuary in the woods behind the farm."

The farmer nodded in response. "Ivy will stay with me, and Kringle is going to my cousin's sheep farm up north. He has a farm near Union and is planning to train Kringle for top level sheepdog trials."

Ella and Caleb followed Mr. Price back into the reception area where their mom, Heidi, and Animal Magic's new veterinary assistant, Jen Andrews, were entering the puppies' details in the computer. Jen had been working at Animal Magic since the beginning of the summer and had quickly settled in.

"And what will happen to Holly?" Ella smiled wistfully as her favorite of the four puppies refused to go back into Mr. Price's well-used pet carrier.

"Yip!" Holly cried, climbing out of the carrier and launching herself from the desk onto the floor.

Caleb lunged at her, but Holly was too quick. She scooted under the magazine rack and hid under the bench in the waiting area.

"She's a firecracker, this one," Mr. Price chuckled. "And she's probably the brightest of the bunch. But she's not going to be put to work. I've promised her to a woman who stopped at the farm the other day to buy a Christmas holly wreath. Her name is Andrea Watson. She lives somewhere in town. To be honest,

I don't know much more than that about her." Mr. Price looked at his watch and realized he had to leave. "Holly's clever, so I hope the Watsons take her to dog-training classes—otherwise, she could be a handful!"

While Caleb went after Holly, Ella fired questions at the farmer. "Have you told Mrs. Watson about training Holly? Does she have a nice big yard? Does she realize that dogs need at least two good walks a day?"

"Whoa!" Mr. Price begged, grinning at Heidi Harrison and holding up his hands in mock surrender.

"I'm sorry about my daughter giving you the third degree, Joe," Mom broke in with an apologetic smile. "Ella worries about every creature in the entire world!"

Mr. Price nodded. "I must admit, I wasn't that happy about giving Holly to Mrs. Watson," he muttered. "But she was insistent, and I agreed."

"Oh, I'm sure it'll work out," Mom said. "And I'll bet that Holly will settle in really well."

"Come on, let's get you back into

the carrier," Caleb said to Holly as he cornered her under the bench and picked her up. This time Holly didn't struggle as he petted her, then snuggled her in beside her sister and brothers.

"Are the puppies fully weaned?" Jen asked Mr. Price for her records.

"Yes. They're eight weeks old, and they're on solid food three times a day," Mr. Price replied.

"And we've given you wormers for them, plus they've had their anti-flea treatment along with everything else." Jen saved the updated file before closing the screen. "That's everything, then. They're ready to face the big wide world. I can print out vaccination certificates and send them to you in the next couple of days."

"Great. That means I can let the new owners know that they can come get them before Christmas." The farmer closed the carrier and picked it up. The puppies yapped and scratched inside.

"Good luck!" Mom called after him, raising her eyebrows at Ella as Mr. Price crossed the frosty yard. "Don't even think about it!"

"What?" Ella faked ignorance.

"I know you, Ella! Don't think about running after Mr. Price and quizzing him again about Holly's new owner!"

"B-b-but…!" Ella hadn't liked the sound of Mrs. Watson—the woman who'd gone to Lakeview to buy a holly wreath, but ended up walking away with a puppy as well. "What if she doesn't know anything about how to take care of a dog?"

"Your worries might be justified," Mom said firmly, watching the farmer put the pet carrier into his truck and drive off. "But it's none of our business, Ella. There isn't a thing we can do."

Chapter Two

The Abandoned Cat

As Mr. Price drove out of Animal Magic with his four adorable puppies, Ella and Caleb's dad drove in. He jumped out of his delivery van and ran around to the back doors. "Can you give me a hand with this cat?" he yelled. "Be careful that you don't slip on the ice!"

"Go get a carrier," Mom told Caleb as she and Ella rushed over to the van.

"I'm sure she's a stray. I found her in the community garden at the back of the post office," Dad explained as he eased open the door. "They're pretty much deserted at this time of year—no one's out there digging when the ground is frozen. The poor creature had been forced to make a den under one of the sheds. I think she would have frozen to death if she'd stayed out much longer."

Mom nodded. "They're forecasting five below zero tonight. And I'll bet that she hasn't eaten lately, either."

"Poor thing!" Ella cried as her mom reached in and gently picked up the stray.

The female cat was a mixture of brown, black, and dirty white. Hardly more than skin and bones, she looked as if she'd given up.

Caleb reappeared with the carrier, and Mom gently lowered the patient in and rushed back to the animal hospital.

"Ella, please go and get a blanket to wrap her in," Mom directed. "We need to restore her body temperature and rehydrate her as quickly as we can. Jen, we'll need to hook her up to a drip." Quickly, Mom took control, fighting to save the cat, who lay on her side without moving. "Someone should give her a name," she suggested.

"Dotty!" The name came to Ella right away.

"Okay, Dotty, you'll feel a small poke," Mom said gently as she inserted the needle to connect her to the drip. "Jen and I are going to take you next door into the cat area and put you under a nice heat lamp. When you're feeling better, we'll give you a more thorough examination."

The cat blinked and took a deep breath. She didn't raise her head as she was carried next door.

"I'll get going on her website entry," Caleb decided, starting to type. "Dotty would love a warm home and a family of her own. Can you give her the care she needs?"

"Yes, that's good. But don't put it up on the site yet," Mom advised.

"I feel so sorry for her," Ella sighed. "Let's just hope that Dad found her in time." Then she remembered something. "Hey, Caleb, did you close the stable door when you came out to see Holly?"

"Uh-oh! I don't think I did."

Caleb and Ella dashed out into the yard, just in time to see Rosie taking advantage of the open door. The shaggy little Shetland pony ventured out into the yard, closely followed by sneaky Chance.

"Stop!" Ella cried, waving her arms and trying to shoo Rosie and Chance back the way they'd come.

The Shetland and the gray foal slid and skidded on the icy surface while Chance's mother, Buttercup, stuck her head over the stable door and whinnied.

"That's right, Buttercup—you tell them

to stop messing around!" Ella muttered, grabbing Rosie's halter and turning her around. "Uh-oh! Here comes Annie!"

Sure enough, her neighbor, Annie Brooks, had been out in her driveway and had heard the clatter of hooves. She and her mom were boarding Buttercup, Chance, and Rosie at Animal Magic until their new stables were finished. Not so long ago, Mrs. Brooks would have been complaining about all the noise, but much to Ella and Annie's delight and surprise, Mrs. Brooks had asked Ella's mom in the fall if Rosie could permanently come and live with them. Annie and Ella hadn't been able to believe it at the time, but now it was clear Mrs. Brooks had a real soft spot for the pony.

"What's going on?" Annie asked Ella.

"Nothing. It's okay. Caleb and I were just about to take these three out into the field to save you the trouble." Ella tried to make it sound as if everything was under control, but naughty Rosie was making it difficult.

"They'll need their rugs," Annie decided, grabbing them from the tack room. "Mom and Dad are out in the field. Dad has taken time off work to finish building the stables. He says they should be ready by Christmas. Mom wants to have a party to celebrate—maybe for New Year's."

"Cool!" Quickly Ella and Annie put on Rosie and Chance's winter rugs while Caleb fastened a halter on Buttercup. Soon they were all on their way to the Brooks's field.

"Hey, Buttercup, look at that!" Caleb exclaimed when he saw Annie's parents hard at work on the wooden stables. "That's five star accommodation for horses!"

Mr. Brooks looked up from his hammering. "Hi there!" he called.

"They look amazing," Ella said, letting Rosie go and walking up the hill

to inspect the stable block. "The horses
are going to love it!"

"And you and Caleb will no doubt
be glad not to have to muck them out
at your place." Mrs. Brooks handed
Mr. Brooks another handful of nails,
then stood back to admire their work.
"They'll be off your hands for good."

"We've loved having them stay," Ella
protested. "We're going to miss them."

"Well, feel free to come and muck out here as often as you like!" Mr. Brooks grinned. "And tell your grandpa to take as much manure as he likes for the plants at his garden center!"

"Will do!" Ella grinned. It was time to go. There was still a ton of stuff to do, including checking on Dotty and putting up a Christmas tree. "Better go!" she said. "See you later!"

Chapter Three
Christmas Excitement

"How's Dotty?" Ella asked Jen as she followed Caleb into the animal hospital.

"She's doing okay," Jen replied. "But it's too early to tell. Your mom thinks we should still wait a while longer before putting her up on the website."

Ella frowned. "That doesn't sound good."

"She's been through a lot," Jen reminded her. "Keep your fingers crossed that she'll pull through."

"Hey, we've got an email from Joel!"

Caleb announced as he signed in and
caught up on the rescue center messages.

Joel had worked as Mom's assistant
before Jen. Now he was in Australia,
working at the main veterinary school
in Melbourne.

"What does he say?" Ella asked.

"Merry Christmas and he hopes we all
have a great time," Caleb reported. "He
says he plans to be back in the States
for New Year."

"Cool!" Ella watched Jen open the
flaps of a cardboard box and pick up
a pale brown rabbit with floppy ears.
"Luckily there's nothing wrong with
young Cocoa here, except that her
ex-owners think she's too much trouble."

Shaking her head, Ella went to pet
Cocoa. She peered into the box. "Who's

this?" she asked, gazing at the matching rabbit still in there.

"That's Peanut, Cocoa's sister. She has darker tips on her ears—see?"

"Cocoa and Peanut," Ella muttered. "What did the owners say?"

"Not much. Just that the family was going away for Christmas and they couldn't find anyone to feed the rabbits. Plus, they've had them for six months and the kids were supposed to groom them and take care of them, but they never bothered, so that's how they ended up here."

"Oh!" Ella went straight to the computer and found the Animal Magic Newcomers file. "Cocoa and Peanut," she typed. "Two fluffy youngsters who need a home together. Are you willing to comb and cuddle them?"

"How does that sound?" she asked Mom, who had just come in from the kennels.

"Perfect. Caleb's already taken their picture. It's very sweet. Before you know it, there'll be a line of people wanting to adopt them."

"We hope!" Quickly Ella clicked through the list of animals on their website. There was Murphy the lively collie cross and Ace the overweight Jack Russell, whose owner had gone into the hospital. Plus Ebony the pretty black cat with pale gray eyes and Flash the outdoor orange cat, who only came home to eat. On and on the list went. *But not many rabbits*, Ella noticed, so they stood a good chance of a quick adoption. *Then again, maybe it would be better for Peanut and Cocoa not to be adopted before Christmas,* she thought. After all, the saying that a dog was for life, not just for Christmas, applied to rabbits, too.

Just then the door opened, and Ella's dad staggered in carrying a tall Christmas tree. "Make way!" he gasped as Ella rushed to hold open the door. "Where do you want this?" he asked Mom.

"Over by the window, beside the magazine rack," Mom said, clearing a path.

"Grandpa chose it and dug it up and put it in a pot especially for us," Dad told her. "He says we're late getting ourselves organized, and this is the best one left in the entire garden center."

"You can smell the pine needles!" Ella loved the build-up to Christmas— getting the box of decorations from the attic, finding out if the lights still worked, straightening up the silver wings of the angel that perched on top of the tree. "When can we decorate it?" she asked eagerly.

"After hours," Mom insisted as the door opened again and another patient came in—an elderly golden retriever who needed to have some teeth taken out. "Hello, Mr. French. Bring Della this way!"

"Busy, busy!" Ella's dad straightened up and rubbed his back. "It's always like this just before Christmas—people suddenly deciding that they can't cope with their pets."

"Yes, I remember last year," Ella said, standing back to admire the tall, straight tree. She tried not to think too much about careless owners who abandoned their animals, and instead looked ahead to tonight—to trimming the tree and wrapping the presents she'd bought for her mom, dad, and Caleb. "I love Christmas. It's so cool!" She sighed. "And there are only four days to go!"

Chapter Four
Trouble Ahead

"This time next week, it'll all be over,"
Jen said matter-of-factly as Ella's dad
dropped her off at the train station early
the next morning. It was three days
before Christmas, and Jen was traveling
home to her family in Canada for the
festive break.

The town was adorned with giant
stars, angels, and Santa Claus
decorations. The streets were crowded
with last-minute shoppers.

"I know—is it worth it?" Dad said with a grin. "We all spend too much, eat too much, drink too much … bah humbug!"

"You old Scrooge!" Ella protested. "I bet you used to love Christmas when you were my age, way back in the olden days!"

"Watch it!" Dad laughed as he helped Jen with her suitcase. "Have a great time, and see you next week."

Jen gave Ella a hug. "Don't forget to drop off those vaccination certificates at Mr. Price's place on your way back," she reminded her. "They're in the glove compartment. He's arranged for the puppies to be picked up today, so he needs them in a hurry."

"I won't forget," Ella promised. She

waved good-bye to Jen as her dad
turned his van around. "That means
you'll get to meet Mr. Price's four
beautiful puppies," she told her dad
eagerly. "There's Jingle and Kringle,
plus Holly and Ivy. They're all going to
be working dogs except Holly."

During the past 24 hours, Ella had
been too busy to think much about the
cute Border collie puppies. But now
she told her dad all about them as
they drove out of town back to Crystal
Park. "Zach Larsen is going to have
Jingle. Kringle is going to be trained
to do sheepdog trials like the ones you
see on TV. That's what I'd do if I was
allowed to have a collie puppy." She
said this slowly to make sure her dad
paid attention, but she got no response.

"They're so clever that they can learn any trick you teach them—they can do obstacle courses through plastic tunnels and over fences and little wooden bridges."

"They're definitely top dogs," her dad agreed.

"And Holly is the best of all. She's got the cutest black-and-white face, with big brown eyes. Her ears kind of fold and flap forward over her face, like someone did origami on them. And her front paws are white with tiny gray speckles—"

"Whoa!" Dad laughed as he took an icy back road up toward Lakeview Farm. "I was wondering why you'd stopped taking care of Dotty and offered to drive into town with Jen and me. Now I know it was because you've fallen seriously in love with one of Mr. Price's puppies!"

Ella sniffed. "Maybe," she admitted. "But honestly, Dad—Holly is so-o-o cute!"

"How is Dotty, by the way?" he asked, changing the subject and turning carefully onto the road up to the farm.

"Much better this morning. Mom had to cut some of the knots out of her fur, so she looks a little scrawny now. But she's a lot stronger. She can stand up while you gently brush her. And she loves being petted."

"That all sounds good," Dad said, parking his van and leaping out. Ella took the certificates from the glove compartment and followed her dad across the yard.

"Hello!" Ella said to a wary gray and white collie who came out of one of the barns to greet them, closely followed by Mr. Price.

The dog wagged her bushy tail in response to Ella's voice.

"This is Tess," Mr. Price told them. "She's the puppies' mother, and a good old dog. Aren't you, girl? This is her third litter."

"We've just come to drop off the paperwork and the puppies' vaccination cards," Dad explained, handing over the certificates as Ella doted on Tess.

"Can Dad see the puppies?" she asked the farmer, hoping to take a peek herself.

"Feel free. They're in the barn, in one of the old cow stalls. You can't miss them."

Ella led her dad into the dark, dusty stone barn, following the sound of lively yapping until they came to a straw-lined stall where Holly, Ivy, Jingle, and Kringle romped and wrestled happily.

"Aren't they beautiful?" Ella muttered. She picked out the two male puppies—already bigger and broader than their sisters. Then she pointed to Ivy. "Mr. Price is going to keep her," she explained.

"So this one is Holly?" Dad asked as the fourth puppy ran to the door and jumped up as if she were on springs. "Look—she thinks you're here to play."

Ella laughed. "She played hide-and-seek in the reception area yesterday—that was after she'd wrestled with the yard brush!"

"I can see why she's your favorite," her dad admitted. "Look at that little face—I'm convinced that she's listening to every word we say!"

Just then, Mr. Price appeared in the doorway. "Mrs. Watson is here to take Holly home," he told Ella and her dad. "Can you get her, Ella?"

With a deep sigh, Ella opened the stall door and slipped inside. Little Holly ran straight over to her and jumped up again. "Hi, Holly. You're coming with me," Ella said quietly. She felt sad as she picked her up. "Say good-bye to your brothers and sister," she whispered.

The puppies yipped and yapped as Ella carried Holly out. "Time to go," she said, sighing again.

"Thank you for calling to tell me that the puppy was ready," Mrs. Watson said to Mr. Price out in the yard. She spoke so fast that it was hard to hear what she was saying. "I'm on my way to drop Lulu off at the kennels and was passing this way."

Still carrying Holly in her arms, Ella paused at the barn door. Mrs. Watson wasn't what she'd pictured. Not that she really knew what she'd been expecting. Holly's new owner was a small, dainty woman in dress pants and high heels.

"Ah, there you are, Holly!" Mrs. Watson exclaimed, turning toward the barn. "Come here, sweetie. We're going to take you home!"

Who's we? Ella wondered, before spotting a small boy sitting in the large car parked beside her dad's van. Then she noticed that he wasn't alone. Beside him sat a huge, gray Great Dane!

"Todd can't wait to get Holly home," Mrs. Watson told Mr. Price. "I promised he could have a puppy as an early Christmas present if he did well on his school exams. He got As in most of his subjects, so here we are!"

Ella pursed her lips. "Good for Todd!" she muttered under her breath. "What's the Great Dane's name?" she asked out loud.

"Lulu. She really belongs to Gina, Todd's sister." Mrs. Watson seemed determined to give them the full family history. "Gina has gone with her father to our house in Canada for Christmas, which is why we're putting Lulu in kennels because she's too much of a handful for Todd and me to handle by ourselves."

Ella wondered why Todd didn't look very cheerful as he sat in the car, staring out at his new puppy. In fact, he seemed to be definitely un-cheerful, sitting beside a dog bigger than he was. The Great Dane seemed equally dejected.

"Todd, come and look!" Mrs. Watson called to her son from the car. Todd opened the door and stepped out slowly. He was about eight, with dark hair like his mom's, and wearing jeans and new sneakers. "He's not used to the countryside," his mother explained to Mr. Price and Ella. "He's a little nervous around farm animals."

"Remember not to spoil the puppy," Mr. Price warned as he gave Mrs. Watson Holly's certificate. "And you too, Todd," he added with a nervous smile as the boy took Holly from the farmer. "No treats from the table. No sleeping at the foot of your bed."

"Just like Lulu!" said Mrs. Watson. "I'm always warning Gina that she spoils her!"

The down-to-earth farmer gave Mrs. Watson a sharp look as if he was having more second thoughts about giving Holly to her. But he was quickly distracted by another car turning into the yard. It was Zach Larsen from Stonybrook.

"Merry Christmas, Zach!" Ella's dad called. "Have you come for your puppy, too?"

A nod from Zach sent Ella running into the barn to get Jingle. "Down, Kringle. Down, Ivy!" she insisted, reaching for Jingle. She closed the stall door and ran back to the yard, clutching the wriggling puppy.

Meanwhile, Mrs. Watson chose that precise moment to get her pet carrier from the car. Lulu seized her chance; she leaped out and broke into a galloping run toward Todd, jumping up and almost knocking him over.

"Watch out, Lulu!" Todd cried as he lost his balance and dropped Holly.

"Lulu, come back!" his mother wailed.

Holly rolled clear of Lulu and Todd, then raced toward Ella and Jingle. "Yip! Yap!" Jingle leaped from Ella's arm, and the excited brother and sister were reunited.

"I couldn't help it!" Todd blurted out before his mom had a chance to scold him.

By this time, Lulu, Jingle, and Holly were running around in the yard, with steady old Tess looking on calmly from the barn.

"I'm so sorry about this," Mrs. Watson said in a helpless, exasperated voice.

"Oh, dear, now I'm going to have a terrible time getting Lulu into the car."

"She's not vicious, is she?" Zach asked, preparing to separate his puppy from Holly and Lulu.

"Not in the least. She wouldn't hurt a fly. But unfortunately, my husband is the only one she listens to. I can't get her to do a thing I tell her. Todd, you pick Holly up. If we get her in the car first, maybe Lulu will follow."

Ella watched Todd and Zach rescue their puppies and carry them to their cars. Meanwhile, Dad and Mr. Price decided to try to grab Lulu.

"This isn't a game!" Dad exclaimed as Lulu turned to lick his face with her long, slobbery tongue. He took her by the collar and held tight. Slowly but firmly, he led the Great Dane to the Watsons' car. "Wow, she's almost as big as Linda's Shetland pony!"

Mr. Price shook his head as the mother and son jumped in after Lulu and quickly drove off. "I only hope I've done the right thing," he muttered.

"Well, at least you can trust me—I'll take good care of Jingle," Zach promised, pocketing his puppy's certificate and wishing them all a Merry Christmas before he drove off.

Ella stood for a long time in the almost empty barnyard. "But honestly, how will Holly handle having to share a home with Lulu?" she said, though she hardly expected an answer. "And what chance is there of the Watsons taking good care of her?"

Chapter Five
A Christmas Eve Crisis

"If you were named Eve, not Ella,
tomorrow we could all say, 'It's
Christmas Eve, Eve!'"

It was two days before Christmas,
and Ella's grandpa, Jimmy Harrison,
made his annual family joke. He sat in
the kitchen at Animal Magic drinking
coffee and eating a slice of pumpkin pie.

"Ha-ha, Grandpa!" Ella wrinkled
her nose. "Isn't it time you made up a
new joke? Anyway, come and see the

Christmas tree in the animal hospital.
Caleb and I decorated it the day before
yesterday. It's cool!"

"Okay, I'm coming, but don't pull me
over!" Her grandfather let himself be
tugged by the hand.

Ella crossed the slippery
yard with him, then
opened the door to
the reception area.
Grandpa stared
up at the tree.

"Wow, it's stunning!"

Covered in tiny white lights and draped with silver balls, with the angel perched precariously on top, the tree took up half the space in the waiting area.

"You chose it for us," Caleb reminded his grandpa from over at the computer. Then he turned to his mom. "Can I put Dotty up on the website yet?"

"Let's wait until after Christmas," she advised. "She's doing well, but I want to keep her here for at least a week so I can make sure there aren't any complications after her hypothermia. And by the way, Ella, have you checked on Della this morning?"

Ella nodded. "I went into the kennels before breakfast. She's still a little tired, but otherwise she seems okay."

"Della was brought in for dental treatment," Mom explained to Grandpa. "But while I was examining her, her owner, Mr. French, mentioned that she had a bladder problem, and it didn't take me long to diagnose a kidney stone. I operated right away and removed a stone as big as a peach."

"Ouch!" Caleb muttered.

"Poor Della. It must have really hurt." Glancing over her brother's shoulder, Ella saw that he had booked an appointment for a Mr. and Mrs. Jackman to come and see Peanut and Cocoa. "What did the Jackmans sound like?" she asked.

"Good. They breed rabbits and are looking for some more flop-eared females. They're coming in this morning at 11," he reported. "I'm going to spruce the rabbits up a bit. Do you want to help?"

"Well," Grandpa cut in. "I can see you're all pretty busy here. Maybe I'll skip the rest of that coffee and come back later."

"No way, Grandpa! We're never too busy for you." Ella grabbed his hand again and led him back across the yard toward the house. "Dad, can you heat up Grandpa's coffee, please?" she yelled. "And if you pour one for Mom, I'll take it back out to her!"

The Jackmans came right on time and fell in love with Peanut and Cocoa. They took them home in a brand-new pet carrier, promising to give the pretty rabbits a fresh start in a loving home. At lunchtime, Mr. French visited Della and was relieved to see that his faithful girl was well on the road to recovery. Soon afterward, Caleb and Ella took two dogs from the kennels on a walk.

Pixie was a tiny greyhound who loved to run off the leash, so Ella let her loose. Rocky was the opposite—a burly but timid boxer who stayed close to Caleb's side.

As they walked by the river, examining the thin layer of ice at the water's edge and wondering happily about the presents they would soon be opening, Annie ran down the field toward them, waving. "Hey, you two!" she began. "Guess what—it's going to snow!"

"Says who?" Caleb asked, bending down to give Rocky a reassuring pat.

The boxer trembled as Buttercup cantered down after Annie, her big hooves thudding over the frozen ground. Rosie and Chance followed more slowly.

"Mom heard it on the weather forecast. It's going to be a white Christmas. And guess what else!"

"Something good?" Ella guessed from her friend's excited expression.

Annie nodded. "Dad finally finished the stables! Buttercup, Chance, and Rosie can spend their first night there tonight!"

As if she understood, Buttercup threw back her head and whinnied.

"Wow, that's cool!" Ella tried not to show that she was sad. "I'll bring their stuff over from our place as soon as I'm finished walking Pixie."

"I'll come over and help you," Annie promised. She pulled her red knitted hat further down her forehead to keep out the biting wind.

"Mom says you can have some special food supplements for Chance that she had in the storeroom at the center," Ella said. "It's his first winter, so he's bound to feel the cold."

"Thanks, Ella." Annie leaned over the fence, suddenly serious. "I mean, really—thanks for everything you've done for Buttercup and Chance—and Rosie!"

Ella gulped back some sudden tears. She was going to miss the horses at Animal Magic! "No problem," she muttered, turning to call Pixie.

"Mom and I will take really, *really* good care of them," Annie promised. "And you can come and see them anytime you want!"

"Three below zero!" Caleb checked the thermometer on the Animal Magic porch.

A starlit night and a frosty morning had passed since the horses had gone to their new stable. It was late afternoon on Christmas Eve, and the faint winter sun had already set. Frost sparkled on the roof and the cobbled yard.

Ella stopped sweeping out the empty stables and peered over the door. "Easily cold enough for snow!" she commented hopefully. A white Christmas would be perfect.

The daily jobs at the rescue center were done—dogs walked, cats fed, small animal cages cleaned—and Mom was finishing up in the hospital when Ella recognized Zach Larsen's old red truck as it pulled up in the yard.

"What does he want at this time on Christmas Eve?" she wondered. "Maybe he ran out of puppy food and the stores all closed early."

"Hi, Zach!" Caleb waved. "What's wrong?"

"It's Jingle. Is your mother around?" Zach asked, hurriedly carrying his limp and seemingly lifeless puppy toward the hospital.

"I'm here," Mom assured him, popping her head around the open door, and beckoning him inside.

Ella and Caleb ran to join them.

"There's something wrong with Jingle," Zach told Mom. "The first thing I noticed was last night—he didn't eat any of his food. I didn't think too much of it at first—I figured it was a delayed reaction to his vaccinations; then this morning, I noticed he had the sniffles."

"Let's take a look," Mom said, carrying Jingle into the examination room. She felt his stomach and peered into his mouth, then took his temperature.

"Not good, is it?" Zach guessed.

"His temperature's sky-high," Mom answered, frowning when the puppy's sides heaved and he let out a dry, hacking cough. "His lungs sound pretty congested, too." She checked his chest with the stethoscope.

"Well?" Zach prompted.

Ella and Caleb watched anxiously. They could tell by the look on their mother's face that she was worried.

"Jingle has the symptoms of something very serious," she told Zach. "It wouldn't be covered by his first set of vaccinations. No—this is very different."

"What is it?" Zach wanted the diagnosis, but Mom wouldn't be rushed.

"The question is, where would Jingle have picked it up?" she wondered. "If it is what I'm thinking, it would be highly infectious. But if it was at Joe Price's place ... surely Joe would have let me know!"

"What is it, Mom?" Ella asked, suddenly afraid for poor little Jingle. The gray and white speckled puppy lay on his side on the sterile blue surface, hardly responding to her mom's thorough examination.

"I'm not totally sure." Mom still wouldn't commit herself. She thought some more, then looked straight at Zach and made her diagnosis. "I think it might be kennel cough," she admitted at last. "And if it is, I'm afraid that's very bad news."

Chapter Six
Turning Detective

"Otherwise known as canine infectious trach-eo-bronch-itis." Caleb went over to the computer and looked up kennel cough. He read his findings to Ella while Mom discussed Jingle's treatment with Zach.

"Canine infectious trach...?" Ella echoed doubtfully, then tailed off.

"Coughing localized to the windpipe and lungs. A respiratory disease caused by several different viruses or bacteria."

"It sounds horrible!" Ella exclaimed.

"Maybe we should put up a warning on the website? You know—'Watch out for kennel cough!'—so everyone realizes it's going around. How do dogs catch it?"

"They can pick it up in any number of places," Mom broke in as she came out of the examination room carrying Jingle. "Dog shows, training classes, kennels—hence its common name, kennel cough. But in fact, they can catch it just by being taken for a walk in an area where another infected dog has been—like a park, or a field. It's often impossible to track down the original source."

"But you think you can cure him?" Zach asked anxiously.

Mom nodded and unlocked the medicine cabinet. "I hope he'll respond

to these antibiotics. I'll also give you a
spray, which will open up his bronchial
passages and help him to breathe more
easily."

"Don't we have to keep him in
overnight?" Ella asked.

"No, but Zach, you should keep Jingle
in complete isolation and change his
bedding daily. Make sure the room where
you keep him is well ventilated. And call
me if you're worried."

"Even on Christmas Day?" the young farmer checked.

"In this job, we never close!" Mom smiled as she opened the door and handed Jingle over to his owner. "Merry Christmas!" she called to Zach. "And try not to be too concerned!"

"So where on earth did Jingle pick up his infection?" Ella asked anxiously. "I'm sure he never even left Mr. Price's farm before yesterday, except to come here for his vaccinations!"

Mom shook her head. "It's a mystery. Like I said, I'm certain Joe would have called me if any dog on his farm had contracted the virus. And he'd have known to keep the animal in strict isolation. This thing can last up to three months, and it's very contagious.

Most kennels won't take a dog in unless it's been vaccinated against kennel cough."

"And what happens if you don't treat it?" Caleb wanted to know.

"There are all sorts of complications— permanent lung damage, for instance. And that can be life-threatening."

"You mean Jingle could die?" Ella asked.

"It's possible. But we've diagnosed it early, and he's getting treatment. It's the dogs who never see a vet who suffer most."

"So we should call Mr. Price and tell him about Jingle right now," Caleb suggested.

"Definitely." Mom picked up the phone and dialed the number of Lakeview Farm. "Hello, Joe? It's Heidi Harrison...."

"And we'll have to call Mrs. Watson,"
Ella remembered. "Mom, please ask
Mr. Price for Mrs. Watson's address and
phone number. We need to find out if
Holly has caught the virus."

Mom nodded. "...Yes, Joe, that's right.
Yes, I'm 95 percent sure it's kennel
cough. Do me a favor and check Tess
and the remaining puppies.... And can
you give me the number for the people
who adopted Holly? ...Oh, I see—yes,
that's a problem.... No, leave it with
me. Call me if you want me to come
out and check on Tess, Kringle, and
Ivy—any time of day or night. Okay,
yes, thanks."

"What happened?" Ella asked as Mom
put down the phone. She could tell that
something was wrong.

"Mr. Price doesn't have Mrs. Watson's contact information anymore. Once she'd picked up Holly, he threw them away. He knows they came from 'town,' but he isn't even sure which one."

"That's terrible," Caleb muttered, closing down the computer. "Now what are we going to do?"

Frantically, Ella thought back to the scene in Mr. Price's yard. She remembered how she'd run into the barn to get first Holly and then Jingle, leaving the other two puppies safe in the cow stall. Then she recalled how Mrs. Watson had opened her car door and let Lulu jump out and run all over the yard. "Mrs. Watson said she couldn't get Lulu to do a thing she told her," she muttered to herself.

"What's that?" Caleb asked.

"I said, Mrs. Watson admitted that she had no control over Lulu, her Great Dane." It all came flooding back to Ella. "That was the reason she was on her way to take Lulu to a kennel for Christmas."

"Good thinking, Ella!" Caleb quickly saw how this would help. "Did she say which kennel?"

Ella shook her head. "But it must be somewhere nearby, because she said she was passing Lakeview Farm on the way there, and there can't be that many boarding kennels around!"

"Here's a list," Mom said, taking a piece of paper out of a desk drawer. "Franklin Boarding Kennels and Crystal Park Kennels are the most likely. Try them first, then go on down the list.

A Great Dane named Lulu shouldn't be too hard to track down!"

"Franklin is a no," Caleb reported after the first quick call. Time was ticking by. Before long, the offices at all the kennels would be closed and wouldn't open again until after Christmas.

"Crystal Park said no, too," Ella reported from the other telephone. "They said they didn't have any Watsons on their books, and no Great Danes, either."

"Okay, I'll try Three Oaks Kennels," Caleb decided, picking up the phone again.

Ella's heart was starting to sink. "Hello, is this Pinewood Kennels?" she asked after she'd dialed a second number.

"Yes, but I'm afraid we're fully booked," the man's voice replied. "We did have one last-minute vacancy, but that was filled this afternoon."

"No, it's okay, I don't want to board my dog," Ella said quickly. "I'm calling from Animal Magic Rescue Center, and I'm trying to track down a Great Dane. I was wondering—do you have one named Lulu staying with you?"

There was a pause before the man replied. "That name rings a bell. Let me check with my wife."

Ella held her breath and waited.

"Yes, I thought so." The man at Pinewood came back to the phone. "That's how our last-minute vacancy came up—a family named Watson had reserved a spot for their dog over the phone. But when they got here, they didn't have any vaccination certificates. The owner said she'd been too busy to get it done. And, of course, we don't take a dog unless the owner can produce the right paperwork. Anyway, I noticed the dog already had a watery discharge from her nose, plus a little bit of a cough."

"So what happened?" Ella asked, hanging on the man's every word.

"We turned them away."

"So Mrs. Watson took Lulu home?"

"That's right. To be honest, the dog looked like quite a handful. I didn't envy the little Border collie puppy she had with her."

Ella's heartrate quickened as she asked the kennel owner one last question. "Can you please give me the Watsons' address and telephone number?"

There was another long pause before the man spoke. "I'm sorry," he replied. "My wife must have deleted their information from the system."

Chapter Seven
A Snowy Delivery

"Look—it's snowing!" Ella's dad told her after dinner. He led her to the kitchen window and made her look outside. "It's like a real-life Christmas card!"

Ella watched big white flakes float down from the dark sky. Already the yard and the rescue center roof were covered in a thick layer of snow.

"Why the glum face on Christmas Eve?" Dad asked gently. "Do you want to tell me what's up?"

"No thanks, Dad. I'm okay."

"No, you're not," he insisted, drawing her toward the fireplace. Mom and Caleb were in the living room, stacking presents under the Christmas tree. "Come on—spill the beans!"

"I can't help worrying about Holly," Ella burst out breathlessly. "Puppies can die from kennel cough. And you know something—I bet Todd Watson and his mom won't know what to do if Holly gets sick!"

"You don't know that for sure," Dad said. "Ella, I know this is really hard for you, but it may be something we can't do anything about. Without knowing which town the Watsons live in, we might just have to let the problem go."

Ella's eyes filled with tears. "But this is their fault. I'm sure Lulu is the one who's infecting the others—the man at Pinewood Kennels said she had a runny nose and a bit of a cough."

Dad sighed. "We still can't help, no matter how much we might want to."

Ella nodded as a tear splashed onto her cheek.

"So we just have to concentrate on enjoying Christmas, okay?"

This time, Ella couldn't even manage a nod. Instead, she sniffed, then said, "I'm going out to check the cat area and say hi to Dotty."

"Good idea," her dad agreed. "Put your heavy jacket on. It's cold out there."

Ella found the little cat curled up and asleep in her warm bed. "You look snug," she whispered.

At the sound of Ella's voice, Dotty opened her eyes.

"I'm sorry! I didn't mean to wake you!" Ella leaned into the unit and petted the thin cat. "Look at your fur— it's all spiky and uneven."

Meow! Dotty stood up and brushed against Ella's hand for another rub.

"There! You're so cute. How did you end up under a shed?"

Meow! Dotty said again.

"Never mind. After Christmas, we're going to find you a wonderful home with a nice family to take really good care of you," Ella promised.

Nearby, other cats meowed for attention, so Ella went down the row, petting them and talking softly. Then, after 10 minutes, she decided it was time to go back to the house. "I'll try to be more cheerful!" she promised Dotty as she took one last look. "After all, it's not fair to ruin everyone's Christmas, is it?"

Meow! Dotty replied, settling down to sleep again.

Ella left the cat unit and quietly closed the door. She turned up the collar of her jacket and stepped out into the snowy yard. Further along Main Street, she heard the sound of carolers:

"Deck the halls with boughs of holly…."

Ella walked across the yard, gazing up at the whirling, ice-cold flakes. Suddenly, she heard footsteps around the front of the house. *Who's that?* she wondered.

Maybe it was one of the carolers running ahead of the others to knock on doors. She went around the side to take a look, but there was no one there.

"That's funny," Ella muttered, spotting scuff marks and footprints in the snow. The footsteps headed to and from the front doorstep. "Weird."

She looked up and down the street—

no, definitely no one there. Then she turned and stopped in her tracks.

There was a small, dark shape on the doorstep. Ella stepped closer to take a look.

The shape moved—a small creature, half covered in snow. She looked again.

"Yip!" the tiny thing cried.

At first Ella couldn't believe what she was seeing. A black-and-white puppy with speckled front legs was shivering and crying on the porch.

"Holly?" Ella whispered.

The collie puppy gave another tiny bark.

"Oh, Holly!" Ella gasped, picking her up and knocking frantically on her own front door. "Mom, Dad, Caleb, open the door quick! It's Holly—she's been abandoned on our porch. Quick, before she freezes!"

"I'll keep her warm by the fire while you go and get the medicine and equipment you need," Dad said to Mom.

Caleb had opened the door and let Ella and Holly in, then the whole family sprang into action. "Yes, we shouldn't take her anywhere near the other dogs," Mom agreed. "She probably has kennel cough, just like Jingle. We'll have to isolate her until the infection is dealt with."

Mom ran across to the hospital while Ella gave her dad a towel to dry the melting snow from a still-shivering Holly.

"I'm going out to look for the person who dumped her," Caleb decided, grabbing his jacket. He left by the front door and ran up Main Street.

"Maybe she found her own way here," Ella's dad suggested after Caleb had left.

But Ella shook her head. "I heard footsteps. There were tracks in the snow." She stood to one side as her mom dashed back in and got to work.

"The same symptoms as Jingle," Mom muttered once she'd listened to Holly's chest. "And this time there's a discharge from her eyes."

Ella's heart beat fast, but she tried
not to panic. "Don't worry, Holly," she
whispered, crouching down to pet her
favorite puppy. "Mom knows what she's
doing. She's a really good vet!"

Poor Holly gazed up at Ella with a
scared look in her dark-brown eyes.

Ella rubbed her fur gently. "Now that
you're here at Animal Magic, you'll
be safe. I won't leave you until you're
better, cross my heart!"

Chapter Eight
The Unexpected Visitor

"It's a total mystery," Caleb reported.
He'd been up and down Main Street,
quizzing the carolers and other passers-
by. "Nobody saw anything unusual—
no cars pulling up outside our house, no
strangers—nothing!"

"Just dumped!" Ella said angrily.
"How cruel is that!"

"Shhh." Mom had finished treating
Holly and now appealed for everyone
to be calm. "What's done is done.

The main thing is that she is receiving good care."

"Poor Holly," Ella sighed, afraid to pick her up, yet longing to cuddle her. The puppy lay on a big cushion, soaking up the heat from the log fire.

Holly took a short breath, then let out a noisy, dry cough. She coughed for so long that Ella was scared she had something stuck in her throat.

"She sounds awful," Caleb muttered.

"Yes, she does, but the antibiotics will kick in soon," Mom told them. "And I'm thinking an old-fashioned remedy might help, too."

"What is it?" Ella said eagerly. She would do anything to help Holly.

"Bring her upstairs. We'll run a hot bath and close the bathroom door. We'll keep Holly in there for 20 minutes so she can inhale the steam. That'll ease the cough."

"Like a sauna," Caleb realized as Ella carried the puppy upstairs.

"I'll sit with her," Ella offered.

All through the rest of Christmas Eve, Ella kept her promise not to leave Holly on her own—first in the steam-filled bathroom, then down in the living room again, settling her back on her comfy cushion and gently patting the tiny puppy's chest as her mom had shown her.

"That's another way of helping the cough," Mom explained.

"I think it's working," Caleb said. "She seems better already."

By bedtime, Ella had made a decision.

"I'm not going to bed tonight," she announced. "I'll stay down here and sleep in a sleeping bag next to Holly."

Her dad smiled. "I'd better let Santa Claus know that you're sleeping downstairs!"

"Da-ad!" Ella giggled.

"It's okay. I'll go get your sleeping bag and pajamas." Her mom laughed. "And we'll find the air mattress for you. Come on, let's get organized. It's late, and I don't know about anyone else, but I'm exhausted."

Fifteen minutes later, Ella snuggled down in her sleeping bag beside Holly, making sure she could see her in the dim light of the dying fire. "Don't worry,"

she whispered as her mom checked the
fireplace one last time, turned off the
light, and closed the door. "Everything's
going to be all right—I promise!"

Outside, the snow kept on falling.
By midnight, all of Crystal Park was
sparkling and silent. Then the sky
cleared. Stars shone and dawn crept in
with a faint, pink light.

Ella woke to the sound of Holly
whimpering. "What is it?" she
whispered, wondering at first where
she was, then realizing she was on a
mattress on the living room floor. The
empty Christmas stocking that her dad
had hung from the back of a chair was
now stuffed with brightly-wrapped
presents.

The little puppy sat up on her cushion,
ears pricked. She gave a sharp yap.

"It's okay, I'm still here," Ella
whispered, surprised that she'd
managed to sleep at all. The last thing

she remembered was drowsily gazing at Holly, who was asleep on her cushion. Now it was almost light—it was Christmas Day!

Holly barked again.

"Shhh!"

"Yip! Yap!" The puppy slid off her cushion and ran to the door.

"Hey, you must really be feeling better!" Ella exclaimed. "But what's bothering you?" Sleepily, Ella struggled out of her sleeping bag and followed Holly. She peered through the window at the snowy yard. "Oh!" she gasped, frozen to the spot with shock.

A small, worried face was peering back at her. The face was full of fear as its eyes met Ella's.

"Todd?"

In an instant, the face vanished. Ella hurriedly unlocked the door. She ran out in her bare feet, just in time to see Todd Watson sprinting away.

"Please let me follow him!" Ella begged. She was back in the kitchen, shoving her feet into her boots and flinging her jacket on over her pajamas. "Mom, I have to go!"

Mom had heard the kitchen door open and came downstairs to investigate. "Follow who? Ella, hang on a minute— tell me exactly what happened!"

"Todd Watson—he was here a few seconds ago, peeking through the window!"

"Are you sure you weren't dreaming?"

"No. Holly heard him creeping around outside. She started to bark. That's why I woke up." Seconds were slipping by. Todd was getting away.

"But what was he doing here at this time in the morning? How did he get here?" To Mom, none of this made sense. She stood in front of the door, blocking Ella's way out.

"All I know is—he was here!"

"What's going on?" Caleb mumbled, appearing at the foot of the stairs, his hair messed up, his face still bleary with sleep.

"Caleb, get dressed!" Ella cried. "You have to help me find Todd. He's just been here, plainly looking for Holly."

"You mean he's the one who dumped her?" Caleb asked.

Ella nodded. "How else would he know she was here?"

"Merry Christmas, everyone." It was Dad's turn to interrupt. He'd followed Caleb downstairs, still half asleep. "Is it time to open presents?"

"Merry Christmas, Dad," Ella said. She was desperate to follow Todd, but her hopes of finding him were fading. "Caleb, hurry up—Todd's getting away!"

"Ella says she saw Todd Watson snooping around the house," Mom explained to Dad. "I know, I'm surprised, too. But I suppose we have to let Caleb and Ella take a look."

Dad nodded.

"Hooray!" *At last!* Ella hurried over to Holly to explain. "We won't be long.

You have to wait here where it's nice and warm. Mom says you have to rest as much as possible!"

Holly wagged her little tail.

"Stay!" Ella held up a warning finger. "I'll see you in a bit!"

Chapter Nine
Following the Trail

"So which way did Todd go?" Caleb
wondered as he and Ella stepped out
into the first light of Christmas Day.

"That's easy—he went past Annie's
house!" Ella pointed to one set of clear
footprints—the only ones to spoil the
smooth covering of snow.

"Let's go!" Caleb cried. "If we hurry,
we can catch up to him."

"He looked pretty scared when he saw
me," Ella said. "He'll be running away

as fast as he can."

"Look—a skid mark—he must have slipped."

"And here's another one." Ella pointed to where Todd's footprints turned down a side street and headed downhill. Her own feet crunched into the crisp snow. "Whoa!" she cried, grabbing the fence as she slid and almost fell.

"The trail is leading us to Riverview Road," Caleb pointed out. "I wonder who Todd Watson knows down here."

Ella shrugged. It was weird being out so early, when all her friends would be jumping out of warm beds and tearing at wrapping paper to see what Santa Claus had brought. "Let's go and find out," she said, following Todd's tracks to the short row of terraced houses overlooking the river. The trail led into the yard of number four.

"Are we going to knock on the door?" Caleb asked. "Won't it look a bit—weird?"

"Who cares?" Ella replied. "All that matters is finding out why Todd dumped Holly on our porch!"

She knocked loudly on the red door and waited.

After a while, there was the sound of someone unlatching the lock, and a woman's head appeared. "Yes?" she asked warily. She was in her nightgown, with white slippers on her feet.

"I'm sorry to bother you," Ella said, trying to peer down the hallway. "We're looking for Todd Watson."

"He's in bed," the woman answered.

"Do you have any idea what time it is?"

Just then, a second woman appeared in the hallway. Ella recognized her right away as Todd's mother. "We definitely have the right place!" she muttered to Caleb, who was hanging back and looking embarrassed. "Mrs. Watson, we need to speak to Todd!"

"As my sister said, Todd's still asleep," Mrs. Watson insisted. "What's this all about?"

"Are you sure he's in bed?" Ella held her ground. "I think you'd better check."

Mrs. Watson stepped out into the porch. "I've seen you before—up at Lakeview Farm."

Ella nodded. "My mom and dad run Animal Magic Rescue Center. Mom did Holly's vaccinations."

"So you're here to check on Holly when you should be at home with your family, enjoying Christmas like everyone else. I think I'd better speak to your parents."

"I'm going to check on Todd," her sister decided, then disappeared upstairs.

"If you must know, I left Lulu and Holly at home," Mrs. Watson told Ella with a cold stare. "A neighbor is stopping by to check on them while we're away."

"But you can't do that, even if it was true!" Ella cried. "Holly has only been with you a couple of days. She's just a puppy. It's not fair to leave her alone like that!"

"But it's not true." Caleb stepped forward with the facts. "Because we've got Holly at Animal Magic."

"That's not possible!" Mrs. Watson gasped.

Her sister ran downstairs in a panic. "Andrea, Todd isn't in his bed!"

Mrs. Watson's hands flew to her face.

"It's been slept in, but he isn't there now!" Todd's aunt confirmed. She looked hard at Ella. "Tell us what's going on!"

"That's what we're trying to find out!" Ella muttered. "Todd was at our place just a few minutes ago, peering in through the window—we followed his trail back here."

"It's obvious he snuck out," Caleb said thoughtfully as Mrs. Watson and her sister started to panic. "And the tracks show that he definitely came back. I bet he's hiding somewhere close by because he's scared...."

"Scared of what?" Mrs. Watson interrupted. "Oh, this is terrible!"

"Wait a second!" Ella's sharp eyes had spotted a trail of water across the hallway tiles. It led to a cupboard under the stairs. "That could be melted snow from Todd's boots."

In an instant, Mrs. Watson had dashed down the hall and flung open the low door. "Oh, Todd—there you are!" she cried, dragging him out. "Oh,

you poor boy—you're shivering. What
on earth have you been doing?"

Ella and Caleb sat at Todd's aunt's
kitchen table, waiting for him to explain
everything. Todd was crying, even
though his mom had hugged him and
told him over and over that he wasn't
in trouble, whatever he'd done. "But
you have to tell us what happened," she
insisted gently. "How did Holly arrive
at Caleb and Ella's porch?"

"You won't be angry with me?" Todd
whispered nervously.

His mom held his hand and shook her
head. "Of course not."

"Okay. I did it because Holly was
sick," Todd confessed.

"Did what?" His Aunt Jackie made everyone a mug of hot chocolate, then sat down at the table to listen.

"I smuggled Holly out of our house in a big bag of Christmas presents—because she wasn't very well and I didn't want to leave her all alone."

"Holly would have been perfectly okay with Mrs. Browning taking care of her...," Mrs. Watson began. Then she blushed and fell silent.

"You didn't even realize that Lulu was sick," Todd went on. "I tried to tell you, but you were too busy to listen."

"So then what happened?" Ella prompted. "After you smuggled Holly out in the bag of presents, what then?"

"Mom drove here to Aunt Jackie's, and I sneaked Holly upstairs. But she was really sick then—coughing a lot—and I was scared."

"So you snuck out and brought her to Animal Magic," Caleb concluded.

Todd nodded. "I'd seen the sign outside the rescue center when we drove past. I left Holly on the porch because

I needed you to take care of her."

"It would've been better to knock on the door," Ella told him. "As it was, it was lucky we found her."

Todd hung his head. "I was going to, then I heard you walking across the yard, and I was scared. Really scared. So I ran away. Is Holly okay?" he asked, wiping tears from his face with the back of his hand. "Is she getting better?"

"Slowly," Ella told him. "She has kennel cough. Mom gave her some medicine, but it'll take a while for Holly to get completely better."

"But you definitely did the right thing, Todd," Caleb added. "If you hadn't brought her to Animal Magic, she might have died."

At this, Mrs. Watson sprang to her

own defense. "I couldn't bring the dogs here, could I?" she appealed to her sister. "There isn't room for Lulu in this tiny house. Besides, it was only for a couple of days."

"And you didn't realize they were sick." Jackie tried to help, but it only seemed to make her sister feel worse. She turned to Ella. "What about Lulu?" she asked quietly. "Does she have this kennel cough, too?"

"We think she's the one who had it first, and she passed it on to Holly and Jingle," Ella replied before turning to her brother. "Caleb, what are we going to do about Lulu?"

"We'll tell Mom," he decided quickly. "Mrs. Watson, will you lend us your house key? Dad will be able to drive

over and bring Lulu back to the rescue
center. But if we're going to help Lulu,
we have to do it now—before presents,
or breakfast, or anything!"

Chapter Ten
The Best Christmas Ever

"See how well Holly's doing?" Ella
said as she led Todd into the kitchen at
Animal Magic. "She's almost back to
normal!"

The puppy stood up and wagged her
tail.

Todd heaved a sigh of relief. "Hi,
Holly. It's me!" He turned to Ella. "Can
I pick her up?"

She nodded, and Todd swept up Holly
in his arms. Through the open door

she could hear Mrs. Watson talking to her mom.

"You can cuddle her, but don't let her get too excited," Ella warned Todd before she tuned in to the conversation in the living room.

"Mark and Caleb shouldn't be too long, snow permitting," Mom was saying to Todd's mom. "The sooner they get back here with Lulu, the better. If she's already had this infection for a few days, there may be other problems that will need to be looked at as soon as possible."

"I see now that I've been terribly irresponsible," Mrs. Watson said after a long pause. "But the truth is—I've been very busy trying to organize everything in time for Christmas without my husband."

"That's okay," Mom said kindly. "You don't have to explain."

"I'm sorry I've made such a mess of taking care of the dogs."

Mom nodded. "Like we always say—people must think long and hard about having pets if they're going to feel tied down by them over the holidays."

"I'm afraid that's true for us—given that we own a house in Canada. I didn't really think about how things would work when I gave in to Gina, who was begging for us to have a dog. As for getting Holly for Todd—it was more my idea than his. I thought he'd like to have a dog of his own and be the same as his sister."

"I can hear Mark's van in the yard." Mom cut the conversation short.

"If you'll excuse me!"

Hearing this, Ella peered through the window.

"Here comes Dad!" she told Todd, leaving Holly with him and his mom and dashing outside. "Do you have Lulu?" she asked Caleb, who jumped out of the van first.

He nodded. "She's really sick—she's gone downhill fast since last night when the neighbor went in to feed her."

"That's what happens with this illness," Mom said. She reminded Dad and Caleb to keep Lulu away from the kennels as they lifted the sick Great Dane out of the van. "Can you carry her into the empty stable block? We'll keep her isolated and make a bed for her there."

Quickly the arrangements were made.
While Mom went to get antibiotics
and a saline drip, Ella ran ahead into
the stables to arrange a bed of straw
covered by a clean horse blanket from
the tack room. Dad and Caleb laid her
down gently.

"She's wheezing badly," Dad warned
Mom when she came back. "And she
hardly has the energy to stand, let alone
walk."

Nodding, Mom began her treatment.

"The problem with this sickness is that there's an organism called mycoplasma involved—a hybrid of both a virus and a bacterium—which means that the antibiotic isn't foolproof."

Once more Ella was caught by a sudden rush of worry. She knelt down by Lulu and petted her softly.

The Great Dane slowly raised her head and nuzzled Ella's hand.

"Let's hope Lulu's immune system is strong enough to kick in and fight back," Mom said, standing up at last. She and Dad made way for Todd and his mother, who had just come into the stable to see Lulu.

They all gazed down at the patient.

"How is she?" Mrs. Watson asked.

"She's doing okay," Mom replied.

"You can stay with her for a while if you'd like."

Todd nodded. He knelt in the straw and petted Lulu.

"We'll be in the kitchen with Holly if you need us," Dad assured the Watsons, leading Mom, Caleb, and Ella out of the stable and closing the door.

Back in the house, Ella grew thoughtful. "Mom, if Holly and Lulu do get better, will they have to go back to the Watsons?"

"Yes, wouldn't it be better if we put the dogs on our website and found new owners who could take care of them properly?" Caleb argued eagerly.

Mom glanced out across the snowy yard. "Lulu and Holly haven't been signed over to us," she pointed out.

Dad agreed. "At Animal Magic, we can't take in pets without their owners' permission."

"True," Caleb admitted.

Ella wasn't convinced. All she could think about was Lulu and adorable Holly. "But the Watsons aren't very good with animals. Holly's been through a lot already—I'd hate to think what else could go wrong!"

"Let's talk about it later," Mom warned as she looked out of the window and saw Todd and his mom appear at the stable door.

Ella sighed loudly.

"At least we can give Mrs. Watson the name of a good dog trainer," her dad suggested. "Then, when Lulu and Holly get better, we'll know they have access to the best possible teacher."

"Hmm," Mom said slowly. She seemed to be deep in thought.

"I bet Mrs. Watson will agree to do that," Caleb said. "She seems pretty sorry about what happened."

Mom patted Ella's arm as the Watsons walked across the yard toward the house. "Mark, let's have a quick word," she suggested. "Wait here," she told Ella and Caleb, swiftly taking their dad outside.

"What's going on?" Ella wondered.

Caleb listened at the door. "I can't hear a word," he told her, going to the window instead. "All I can tell you is that Mom and Dad have finished talking and decided to have a chat with the Watsons!"

"I'm still worried, Caleb. I wish we could wave a magic wand and change the Watsons into perfect dog owners!"

"If only!" he sighed.

Together they watched their mom and dad having a long talk with Mrs. Watson. Todd listened quietly, nodding whenever his mom turned to ask him a question. He waited patiently as she took out her cell phone and made a long call. Then at last, Todd and his mother walked with Mom and Dad toward the house.

"Caleb and Ella, Todd has something to say to you," Mrs. Watson announced as all four came into the kitchen.

Ella held Holly safe in her arms, feeling her rough pink tongue lick her fingers.

"Thank you very much for saving Holly," Todd began.

"And thank you!" Ella said softly.
"Bringing her to Crystal Park with you
was what really saved her life."

Todd swallowed hard. "Your mom and
dad and my mom have been talking
about Holly and Lulu," he went on.
"Mom has decided that it would be best to
put Lulu on the Animal Magic website."

"You mean—you want us to find her a new home?" Ella gasped. She guessed that Todd was bravely holding back the tears. "And do you think so, too?"

He nodded. "We called Dad and Gina, and they agreed that we weren't taking care of Lulu very well."

"She needs a house with a bigger yard and someone who can take her for long walks," Mrs. Watson explained.

"When she gets better, can you find her somewhere like that?" Todd asked Ella and Caleb.

"You bet!" Caleb said quickly, while Ella stared at Todd in surprise. "Shhh, stay still, Holly!" she muttered as the puppy wriggled on her lap.

"And what else did you want to say, Todd?" his mother prompted.

"We haven't taken care of Holly very well, either," he said miserably. "She was having a great time with her brothers and sister at Lakeview Farm, and ever since she came to our house, she's been sad."

"Wait! What are you saying?" Ella gasped. She glanced at her mom and dad, who had on their "Don't ask us!" expressions.

"Do you mean you want us to find a new home for Holly, too?" Caleb asked excitedly. "A home in the country, where she has space to run around and herd sheep and do all kinds of sheepdog things?"

There was a long pause while Ella held tightly to precious Holly.

"Not exactly," Todd said with a frown.

"What then?" Ella asked, leaping up.

Todd came to stand close to her and the puppy. "We'd like you to keep Holly," he muttered.

"Me?" Ella said faintly.

"You and Caleb," her dad said, watching her face slowly light up. "Your mom and I talked it through, and we both agreed to break our golden rule of no family pets."

"Just this once!" Mom warned. "Since you're so fond of Holly, and this is a very special case."

Ella went over to Caleb. "Did you hear that?" she said excitedly.

Caleb took the puppy in his arms. He nodded.

"Caleb is too happy to speak!" Dad laughed. "So, what about you, Ella? Do you think it's a good idea?"

"Pinch me, somebody, and tell me it's true!" she cried. She beamed at Todd. "Don't worry—Holly will live here with us, and you can come and see her whenever you want!"

"How about right after Christmas dinner?" Dad suggested with a wink.

Todd nodded eagerly. He watched Caleb set Holly down on her cushion by the fire, then looked out across the yard, past the stables to the fields beyond. "She's going to love it here, isn't she, Mom?"

"Definitely," Mrs. Watson agreed. Then quietly she took Todd's hand and led him toward the car.

"This is the best Christmas ever!" Ella cried.

The turkey was roasting in the oven, the presents were opened, and wrapping paper lay scattered all over the living room floor.

Caleb laughed as Holly got tangled up in red ribbon, then pounced on Ella's bag of chocolates.

"Merry Christmas, everyone!" their

grandpa called as he opened the door and kicked off his snowy boots. There was an inviting smell of Christmas dinner, newly opened packages … and chaos in the kitchen. "My goodness! What's going on here?"

Ella flew to greet him. "Grandpa, guess what happened!"

"Did Santa Claus come?" he asked with a twinkle in his eye.

"Better than that," Caleb said, a grin spreading from ear to ear.

From under a large piece of silver wrapping, Holly made a sudden pounce at their grandpa's feet. She growled and crouched down, ready to attack his thick, gray socks.

"Mom and Dad have broken their rule!" Ella cried, bending to pick Holly

up and cuddle her. She and Caleb had
a puppy of their very own—it was a
dream come true. "Holly is going to live
at Animal Magic. She's ours—to keep!"